A CAGE WITHOUT BARS

Also by the Author

In the Middle of Nowhere

Watching from a Distance

Ibrahim Yared

A CAGE WITHOUT BARS

Saqi Books

British Library Cataloguing-in-Publication Data
A catalogue record for this book is available from the
British Library

ISBN 0 86356 502 6

First published 2003 by Saqi Books

Saqi Books
26 Westbourne Grove
London W2 5RH
www.saqibooks.com

Contents

Preface

Isolation is not the choice of a human being ... it invades his life quietly.

Following its different manifestations leads one into a labyrinth of dreams and realities, ending up in a cage without bars that is not noticed by others.

Oddly enough the cage changes with changing situations, it has different sizes and the absent bars have a new design in every case.

Prologue

The small boy was trying to climb over the wall surrounding the labyrinth that he wanted to leave, when he heard the elderly people back home shouting and telling him to go back to bed. His grip on the wall loosened and he fell to the ground waking up from his dream to find himself – seventy years older – in his usual armchair at home watching the people around him involved in their busy discussion.

His problem of not hearing well sometimes placed him in a cage without bars whenever he happened to be in a big group.

The dream in the labyrinth put on different masks; he waded through different surroundings crowded with people who – having different problems themselves – ended up by facing the same isolation which, to different degrees, left them politely ignored by the others. Coming out of the labyrinth he found out that whatever realities were in his dream, they had evaporated.

All the same, the beauty in life does not evaporate ...

He remembered what an old professor, who suffered atrociously from cancer at the age of 80, wrote to a woman friend: 'Life at my age is not easy, but the spring is magnificent and so is love!'

The isolation of his inner world did not influence his daily life but it took him to strange places that existed only in his mind; sometimes they were pleasant, at other times they were sad. In any case, it was not usually noticed by the others and his relations with people continued as before.

Labyrinth

I

All through his life, from childhood to old age, Abe led another life parallel to his real life.

His original life – school, university, work, marriage, children and grandchildren – was happy and successful. He had no reason to complain and his relationships with the people around him developed normally.

His parallel life was all spent in a labyrinth that was endless, having neither an entrance nor an exit. He felt at home in this labyrinth where he followed winding roads, passing by countless homes, sometimes returning to places he had visited before to find them already changed.

His roaming around was not guided and the people he came across belonged to different ages. He was going back and forth without any chronological order.

During his roaming he entered a home where he found himself trying to write the story of a man busy writing the story of another man writing about a third man lost in an effort to write anything final.

II

It was 5 p.m., the sunset was nearly over and Abe was already settled in the retreat of his old age. This retreat was situated in the lower floor of the labyrinth in which he spent all his parallel life. The lower floor was not visible to the people in the labyrinth who did not notice its existence. He used to go up to the upper floor whenever he wanted to turn back the pages of his life to relive any of the events that had passed in it.

For him the scenery of the lower floor was completely different from that of the main floor. The scenery of the main floor unfolded with the corresponding years he was turning back; even the same landscape looked different according to when he was watching it.

Turning back the pages, he met many people. In one of his wandering journeys, he came across the small boy, the teenager and the young man he had been in the past, all scattered in different rooms of the labyrinth.

In one of the rooms he came across his father involved in writing a long explanation of the New Testament. His father, who was practically a stranger to Abe, was too busy with his work and did not want to be interrupted by a voice from the future. Abe started asking his father: 'Are you really here? How can I talk to you? Remember me wherever you are!'

During his wandering he met an old pastor of a church he used to attend as a small boy. The pastor saw in him the young boy he had known and started to ask him about his worries. Abe discovered that he was again the schoolboy who was bothered by the possible outcome of the war (it was the beginning of the Second World War). The worries of that period were so disturbing that he woke up from his dream in the labyrinth to find himself again in his real life.

He felt the passage of a thief who entered his labyrinth treading quietly to take his dream, fold it and put it away in his bag.

III

At night the retreat on the lower floor was more like a stranger's. He used to wander through the different rooms inspecting the place. The furniture resembled that of his home in real life. The original furniture was meant to last a lifetime ... what life? Actually it changed very often.

He was intrigued by a fact that had no specific date. All through their lives, Abe and his life companion were trying to improve their home and decorate it, adding new items they acquired during their trips or whenever they changed their residence. At a certain date, which he could not specify, Abe – at least – stopped being interested in adding new things. He was bothered by the fact that sometimes he did not even notice new items added by his wife. Besides her work teaching and writing, his wife was always keen on arranging things at home, on having flowers all over the place and he felt there was something wrong with him for not planning to stay there forever!

The various possessions floated in their own world, detached from him, and he was wondering what might be worth keeping and eventually be left behind. Left for whom? Were there any memories among the pieces of furniture? Any memories to be cherished? Every item reminded him of the time they had acquired it, the relationship it had to each of his children, the precautions they took to make it last forever … These memories belonged to him and his wife; their children had their own possessions which they cherished and what was left by their parents could have value even without holding the memories that were so dear to those leaving them …

The thought took him out from the lower floor, across the years, to the funeral of the mother of his friend Charles. The mother's home was beautiful but there was nobody left in it. Charles told him that he and his brothers had their own beautiful homes and he did not know what to do with all the furniture his mother was leaving. Their conversation was interrupted by numerous people arriving to pay their condolences and Abe never knew what happened later.

During his wandering, he saw the old homes of his childhood. What had become of them? Even his children did not know what they were like.

One thing was stuck in his memory of the oldest house. It concerned the big paintings hanging on the walls. There were the portraits of his father and the two uncles who had died before he was born. There were also portraits of certain world rulers during the First World War and he never knew what they were there for.

At a certain age, it became more difficult to turn back the pages that took him to the old homes of his childhood. They were in a country that he did not visit for many decades.

What happened to his neighbours there? The colleagues at school and university? The young girls who were a part of his dreams and experiences? Those people who had an important role in his early life, were they still alive? Did they move to different countries? How did he know what had changed and what remained the same? Thinking of these people reminded him of having seen their children who, fifty years before, were starting to walk. Would they know anything about him or his children?

Remembering the places where he was brought up took him to a world he knew very well, although he did not identify with it anymore.

In that past, time was completely frozen and the apprehension of forgetting started to bother him.

IV

Turning back the pages during his wandering, he reached a familiar scene more than half a century back, when the god of chance made him first meet his wife. He had already started his career and she was in her final year at university. A couple of their friends had invited them to an outing on a small boat on the river. He still had the photos taken during that outing

University colleagues, 1946.

When the God of chance made him meet his wife, 1948.

which showed the young man and girl – who had met for the first time – looking from the photo at the old people they would become without being distracted by the passage of time. He could still remember the discussion he had with her about his lack of belief and her belief that turned into a secular attitude later on.

They met many times during the following weeks and it did not take him long to propose to her during another outing on the same river, but this time they were alone. They moved to his parents' country to reside there and got married after a few months.

A very clear view from that period accompanied him all his life.

He felt the wide gap between his childhood and her childhood. She had a big family with many children of around her own age. He had a very small family living in immigration with no relatives around. The cousins of her own age were present all through her life. They moved to different countries as they grew up, but their presence was always in the background irrespective of the relations she had with them. It was always a pleasure to watch the customs they had at different times of the year and the celebrations they made for different occasions and especially for the children they had later on. These customs continued to be practised even after the children grew up and left their parents' homes.

In old age she was happy to get in touch with a number of her cousins who were living in America. The passage of years had no effect on their relationship. She got to meet a number of their children and it felt great to find those children close to her.

His small family did not grow, even after he regained his native country. The relatives he met at an older age did not become a part of his inner world although a number of them became very close to him.

Her company started making him familiar with classical music and world literature. He was already quite well read, but he started seeing in himself the small boy doing his best to get to know as much as he could of world literature. He watched that boy going to the municipal library looking for books to read without any guidance, walking aimlessly in the labyrinth of his young years deciding for himself what to choose. At the time he knew nothing about classical music, she introduced him to a new world and that went on all their life. Fifty years later – when they had attended together many performances of symphony orchestras – he could not forget the first time she had initiated him into that world … and it made him happy.

During their early married life he was taken aback by the difference in their attitude. He was always living with the trauma of his father and uncles leaving the home country at the beginning of the century to avoid the problems in the Ottoman Empire. The sense of insecurity that accompanied him from childhood did not go away even after having had a successful career and a happy family. A funny incident forty years later confirmed his feelings of insecurity. He was always double-checking on everything he did. Once, upon arriving at the office he locked the car and, after walking away ten steps, he went back to check that it was locked. His son who was watching from the balcony could not help making fun of this habit of double-checking …

At the same time she was living with the trauma of losing her country after the Second World War and she always felt the need to do something about it. He did not forget his feeling of unease about her impulse to do something compared to his habit of avoiding any fight. Actually nothing was done about it; the difference in their attitude during that period did not lead to any misunderstanding and, in spite of what was involved, their happy life continued with all the hard work and the feeling of mutual need for each other.

Their children accompanied all their dreams and memories.

V

There was also the memory of sitting next to the driver in an ambulance taking his mother in-law to the hospital where she passed away. All the way there he heard the siren of the ambulance and the heavy snoring of the old woman during the last hours of her life. The sound of the snoring took him back many decades to think of what he was told about her life before he got to know her.

Her suffering during the last months was physical because of her disease, and moral because of her being without work. The woman had been very active all her life. She had started to work in the press of an American mission after finishing high school and she took it upon herself to make sure that her sisters had a proper education. This took place during the First World War.

In her country, which was part of the Ottoman Empire,

The old woman at work, 1955

many families could not receive the mail from their children residing in North and South America. So the immigrants sent their letters to the American mission with whatever money they could afford. This active woman, after work, took the money with her to deliver to the families of those immigrants. Decades later, Abe heard many stories of very old people who could not forget the service she had rendered them at a time when the country was going through a famine.

After getting married to a man from a neighbouring country, she did voluntary welfare work with the same energy. This continued without interruption until her husband died. She returned to her home country and started working in the administration of a hospital to be able to continue the education of her young son, who then travelled to study in Germany, finished his studies, started working in an international firm, got married and remained abroad.

It was at the beginning of this period that Abe, who was already married to her eldest daughter, got to know her and he watched her activity during the following two decades. Upon retiring, she went abroad to visit her son and grandchildren for two months and on her return went straight to hospital for a serious operation. Arriving at the airport she had her usual smile and, somehow, she looked much closer to all of them. Her independent existence had reached an end.

After the operation she could not resume her active life and the family felt that she could not live without work. Closing up her home and moving to live with her daughters was a very painful moment for her. The next phase of her life was less than a year. She spent the last three months suffering in bed refusing to take painkillers. It was at the end that Abe accompanied her in the ambulance to the hospital.

When they reached the hospital, Abe stopped thinking of her past to watch the activity of the medical staff as they put her in a room for intensive care. He did not hear the snoring any more and, when the doctor told him what he was expecting to hear, he called his wife to give her the news and went back home.

He remembered the close relations of his mother-in-law with his children as well as her encouraging attitude when he had had his cancer operation ten years before. At the time Abe was passing through a difficult period. Her presence was reassuring although she did not interfere in his personal life. Now, after so many years, he still saw the smile on her face as she made him feel her support without saying anything.

During the last two decades of her life she was always active, doing her best to help the people around her with their problems and to find jobs for those without work. Her attitude towards her daughters was rather complex and she kept her independence without giving up the need to be close to their lives.

As for her social life during that period, it was limited to her family and her grandchildren were the source of her happiness. Abe still remembered the shining smile on her face – during the last week of her suffering – when her granddaughter, who had a broken leg after an accident, entered the room to see her. After her death, the granddaughter insisted on accompanying Abe to the cemetery when he went to watch the workers digging the ground to prepare a place for the coffin.

No words were exchanged during that visit and all that Abe remembered was the young girl, with callipers on her broken leg, moving slowly among the other graves trying to read the inscriptions on their head stones.

When Abe started seeing his mother-in-law in the labyrinth after that, she was silent but the smile never left her face. She was always in a hurry going to different places to do small things for people who needed her help. It did not look as if she recognized him and he did not try to approach her.

VI

In one of the alleys of the labyrinth, he came across a crowd of people singing in loud voices. Upon coming nearer to the crowd, he discovered that it was composed of different groups, each singing its own praise. None of them cared to hear the others and the praise followed personal and regional lines. They did not have a common subject and each group raised its voice to overcome the singing of the others.

Every group had its writers, poets, actors, painters and musicians – all offering the new books they had published, reading the latest poems they had composed, acting in the different plays written by their writers, painting the scenery of their dreams and playing the music composed by their group. Whenever Abe came across any of these crowds at a later period, he found out that members of the same group – growing older themselves – had changed their singing and looking back to the past, they were anticipating with fear the arrival of the younger generation of their own group.

Mixing with the different groups led Abe to discover a number of individuals who did not really belong to any of them. These individuals had their own subjects and the praise they were singing concerned their own work. Some of them were trying their best to impose their work on everybody else and it was useless trying to talk to them about anything outside the limits of what they were producing. Others were busy producing their work, but they didn't try to impose it on others. They simply did their best to market it and were happy to come across any sign of recognition.

VII

The cage without bars that enclosed him all through his parallel life was always there and he had a feeling of floating down a river watching all the rubbish from his life – the good as well as the bad – sinking slowly every day. This feeling reminded him of a poem written by Emily Dickinson in the second half of the nineteenth century starting with:

> Because I could not stop for Death–
> He kindly stopped for me–
> The Carriage held but just Ourselves–
> And Immortality.

The reflections about death and immortality were the heart of this poet's inner world. Since the age of twenty-five, she had settled into a quiet pattern of life seeing fewer and fewer people and drawing gradually into isolation. At a certain period of his life, Abe was interested in reading the poems of a number of poets of the nineteenth and twentieth centuries, attracted by their suffering.

Thinking of death took him to a different place where he saw his grandson – who was six years old – crying bitterly after the death of his turtle. The boy got very busy, together with his mother and grandparents, burying the turtle in the garden. The big problem was digging a small place for the box of the dead turtle with all the snow and ice covering the ground.

VIII

He watched, in his old age, the country where his children had lived during their postgraduate studies. What he felt had nothing to do with their happy times there, and they did not see how he felt estranged by the places. When he started staying more often with his children in their country of immigration, two decades later, he went to the same cinemas, the same theatres, the same restaurants with them or on his own and what he saw looked different from what they saw. Switching back fifty years to his university days, he felt the same estrangement.

Where was he going? Towards what? Towards the next day, and then? The fact is, he did not know what he wanted or should ever have wanted and he did not even expect to know!

IX

Looking around him in the labyrinth, he saw an endless number of things that reminded him of people who were not there any more. What of the things he was going to leave, would they remind others of him when he was there no more?

Associating certain objects with a human being does not depend on the value of these items, nor does it depend on his attachment to them. It is simply due to certain passing happy or unhappy moments when his inner world seems to be expressed by these objects, whether he feels that or not.

On the Way Out

I

Telling anybody's story saves the narrator from a deep loneliness that is part of the human condition. The search for meaning – in life – raises the possibility that there may be no meaning. These stories bring back things barely remembered, things released only by the act of writing. When the writer goes back, he feels that an age – a vanished adolescence, a disappearing maturity – unites him with the people back there.

II

When Abe and his wife were in a motor-boat cruising the quiet lake, it was not easy to communicate with the old professor at the steering wheel. The man had invited them, together with their relatives whom he knew, to enjoy the tour. It was difficult with the noise of the motor to keep up any conversation, especially as they had nothing in common to discuss, besides the fact that Abe – with his hearing problem – needed a quiet atmosphere to be able to discuss any subject.

The story of the old professor living in a southern part of the United States sounded like leaves blown in the wind. He had come from South Africa for his postgraduate studies and, upon graduation, accepted an offer to stay and teach at the same university. Giving the reason for not going back to his home country, the man explained with a wistful look in his eyes that – at the time – he did not approve of the system of apartheid there, but – at the same time – he could not see himself tolerating the idea of living under the rule of the native people of the country. So his choice was to take the easy way out. He married a European woman who worked with him. Their children were grown up and living on their own in other states. Upon retiring, he acquired a spacious home on the shore of the lake. The place was quiet and peaceful. It did not invade his isolation and allowed him to spend the time reading and navigating his motor boat.

The wistful look was still in his eyes; there was no end to what he managed to read but he did not keep all the books he had bought. Rereading any of them would deprive him of the chance to read new ones and eventually find an answer, any answer, to the questions that no doubt bothered him all his life. These questions were not always the same, they changed with the different phases of his life, with the development of his work and the growth of his family.

It was hard for him to think back so far, to imagine that accumulation of months and years. For these two old people the years had passed, they had seen the job through and the job had seen them through. They both inhabited the same atmosphere of solitude and were just killing time till time got around to doing the same to them.

III

The story of the professor from South Africa reminded Abe of Bengt, a Swedish engineer who had worked with him on a big project thirty-five years before. The man was happy when the head office of his company delegated him to work on a project in a country far away from the snow in his homeland. Bengt was keen on explaining his attitude towards the weather in his country and he got the chance to do it when Abe was on a short visit to the head office in the middle of winter. It was dark, very cold and the snow covered the streets. Coming out of the office at the end of the day, the man left his car in the parking lot of the building and proposed going back to the hotel on the subway. He did not say anything on the way but, upon reaching the hotel and considering that his reason for running away from the weather in his country was clear, he asked Abe whether he had noticed anybody smiling in the crowd!

They became very friendly and Bengt and his wife started going out with Abe and his wife to the nightclubs in town. The popular songs of that period always accompanied the memory of Bengt and his wife.

This couple also had grown-up children who lived in different countries leaving their parents in their secluded life.

Talking about the films they liked to see, Abe told them that they had seen practically all the films directed by Ingmar Bergman. He was taken aback to hear the man saying that he had not seen a single one of them. Bengt explained that Bergman's father was the pastor who had celebrated their wedding and he knew that the pastor did not approve of what his son was doing! Many years after Bengt's death, Bergman directed films about his father and the development of their relationship.

After finishing the project they worked on together, Bengt took a job in North Africa and his wife felt very estranged there. A few years later, Abe received a letter from her that sounded as if she was on the brink of madness. Her husband had died suddenly and she did not know what to do with herself – the formalities to do before taking the body home were endless and there was nobody to help her. Abe tried to contact her but it was useless. Trying to look her up the following summer in Sweden she was not at their old address and that was the last thing Abe knew about her.

One of the outstanding memories Abe still retained showed the very wide gap between the civilization of their two worlds. When Bengt was preparing to leave the country, after having finished his work, he wanted to take with him a souvenir. Abe took him to a big market showing all sorts of crafts produced by the local population and chose for him a collection of glass balls of different shapes and colours. The balls were not all of the same size and the glass which was blown on primitive furnaces was full of small air bubbles that the local population considered a source of pride while showing them to foreign tourists. Bengt could not see anything beautiful in them and the only comment he made was that he considered these products 'A failing attempt of an industry to produce coloured balls!' On going back to his country, he sent Abe a collection of modern crystal balls!

The snow covering the streets of his country, which he never liked, did not leave his spirit.

IV

Many of the people Abe came across were wading through their own worlds of problems, led them to isolation behind different masks.

There was the elderly man who was practically retired when he suffered a stroke. After lengthy treatment, his state of health allowed him to talk, move around and handle his property by himself. His children were adult professionals who had their own families. The only problem was that he did whatever he was involved in slowly. In the mad rush of everyday life, he was politely ignored by others. This led him into a world of isolation and he developed the habit of talking very little, thus creating his own world that nobody cared to inquire about.

Whenever Abe thought of that discouraging experience, the problem of the man's brother came up to dilute the picture. The brother – who was active in the Red Cross – was kidnapped during the civil war. He was never found and no news about his being killed reached his family. What our man felt in his isolation never came out. It was interesting for Abe to try communicating with the man during their rare meetings, but the presence of other members of the family made the attempt pointless and the subjects they talked about were far from the man's inner world.

Again there was the middle-aged man who was a successful engineer with activities in a number of countries in the Middle East. His children were teenagers and he had many relatives around him. He had a stroke and the long period of treatment did not help to make him walk again. He was stuck in his wheelchair with just one arm moving normally but his mental capacity remained intact. He could manage to prepare the designs ordered by his clients from neighbouring countries, always at home working at his computer.

The isolation started to weigh on him when the work fell off and, being unable to travel or run around looking for new projects, he felt trapped in his hole. The economic crisis struck him more when the last few clients took the work he had done for them without paying him his fees. His friends and colleagues dropped in to see him from time to time but they had their own problems to worry about. In spite of his problem, he repeated with a sad smile that there were cases much worse than his! Whenever Abe passed to see him there was a reciprocal understanding between the two worlds of isolation and the man started coming out of his inner world.

The man's wife, who had an extrovert character, did her best to help him. She tried to keep a pleasant atmosphere going but it was not that easy. Their situation and the dwindling number of friends and relatives they saw had a negative effect on her and the optimist attitude she had gave way gradually to a mature acceptance. Her job teaching young children was of great help.

Their children were doing well at school but their elder son could not overcome his feeling of revolt; he didn't see why he should be deprived of all that he had before his father's sickness. Ultimately they sent him to continue his studies abroad far from the world of his father.

The man's inner world did not come out to communicate with the outside world and he was helpless, having no solution to the problem.

V

Palme was one of the people that Abe knew well. He was living alone with his mother and looked after her until she was too sick to be left alone at home while he was taken up by his job teaching at university. He put her in a home for elderly people. She wanted to be back home but he could not manage on his own. Every afternoon, after coming back from university he would spend some hours with her giving her the evening meal. She felt very happy during those hours and was always waiting impatiently for his coming.

During those visits, he watched her getting gradually older. While caressing her hands, he noticed that they were losing their colour and that the veins in them looked more swollen.

She introduced him to an old woman in the room next to hers. That woman was very pleasant and always made fun of Palme not being married. Her children were well off and they had rented for her a luxurious room in the home. Once – arriving earlier than usual – Palme noticed that she was crying bitterly in her room but, on discovering his presence, she came over and started chatting with him as usual.

Before leaving, Palme passed by the nurse in charge of that floor to ask her whether there was something wrong with the old woman. The nurse started by being evasive but finally she told him that the woman's children, who were living in the same town, never came to see her. They were always inquiring about her needs and were prepared to finance them, but they avoided coming to see her. The only answer they had for the nurse was that they did not know what to talk to her about.

During that period, Palme's life was revolving around his work and the daily visits to his mother. Palme looked relaxed telling his mother's story and her slow journey leaving this world. He was always watching the degeneration of her health, which seemed to captivate his attention.

His isolation during that period became less pronounced after his mother passed away. He married a pleasant professor who helped him to reconstruct his social world.

And life went on.

VI

The last time that Mira – who was quite overweight – went for her kidney dialysis, the orderly helping her let her slip and she broke her leg. Mira had been going for the dialysis sessions three times a week for the previous four years, her children were all abroad and it was surprising for Abe to discover her positive attitude towards her problem. The last accident gave her great uncertainty about the worth of life, everything she had known shrank and she started to play with this shift of scale, to compare what existed in her memory, from childhood and adolescence, with what existed now. Nothing took place in bed but sleep, or no sleep. She tried not to think too much. Like many other things now, thought must be rationed. Thinking could hurt your chances and she intended to last.

One of her daughters was a senior correspondent for an internationally known newspaper. She travelled a lot and was always sent to countries having serious problems and where the fighting was covered by all the world agencies. The newspaper stories were like dreams to Mira, bad dreams dreamt by others. They were too melodramatic, they had dimensions that were not the dimensions of our lives. We were the people who were not in the papers. Mira lived in the blank white space at the edges of the print. It gave her more freedom to live in the gaps between the stories, but these gaps became too tight for her after the last accident.

The sick person – that is you Mira, you have now entered the scene – was lying on her bed. After every bout of pain she would wake up with all the wondering questions about her destiny.

Contrary to plants, which have no memories and cannot remember how many times they have done all this before, she remembered and went on asking herself the same questions about the final issue of her suffering. For a moment, she lost the thread, it was hard for her to remember, but then she did.

In her isolation, she could not see the sense in being alone without her children, making meaningless orbits between her home and the dialysis centre with all the void around, yet she did not see any other alternative and continued to hold on. Her eldest son was around fifty, he had a good job and, like his sisters, he was not married. Her second daughter was involved in medical research. Each one of them was living far from the other and they were always contacting her by phone.

Her last accident left them all at a loss not knowing what to do. In fact the solution was clear, but nobody wanted to consider putting her in a home for elderly people. Her mother had lived in such a home without being sick until she passed away. Then, they all dropped in to see her whenever they were in the home country and it was not easy for them to consider repeating the experience. At the time, Mira was also travelling like them and did not find it abnormal to leave her mother in that home. Now they all avoided thinking of doing the same but, in their subconscious, they knew it was coming. They did not talk about it with Mira who had started to suspect that it was on the way. The memory of her mother was less painful, she had a group of acquaintances in that home and she was not confined to her room, but the isolation was the same and one did not have to discuss it with others. Ultimately she might have to give in to a mature acceptance.

The monotony of her life was interrupted suddenly. The eldest son had a heart attack and died suddenly. All the family came to attend the memorial service and Mira started wondering about the meaning of her life. When everybody left to go back to work, the void around her started shaking her capacity to hold on.

VII

The couple, who had no children, did their best to make the visit enjoyable for Abe and his wife. Going around the house, Abe felt uneasy without knowing why. The house was nicely arranged, there were many interesting paintings by Spanish and African-American painters on the walls, the pieces of furniture were well chosen, there were gadgets everywhere and the table was properly set for all the meals. The couple, who were retired, took them around the area and showed them the exhibitions as well as the nice restaurants in the small town. They also described the trips they took frequently around the world and showed them the acquisitions they had collected during these trips. All the same, the feeling of unease was there and Abe started wondering whether there was something wrong with him, being unable to join the crowds of people always looking to the future.

He could not run away from wondering about the utility of all that he saw. Where did it lead? Who would step into their places sooner or later? Did they feel they would be leaving the world one day? If they did, would they be doing things differently while seeing the ghost around the corner waiting patiently for the end of their trip?

The couple continued to improve their home without taking into consideration the inevitable end of that trip. The woman was always acquiring beautiful jewellery. At the same time, she was looking after her husband whose health posed many problems, all without interrupting the rhythm of their busy life and travels. In between the trips she kept herself busy doing her household activities and reading detective novels.

That stay reminded Abe of the endless number of people completely taken up by their busy daily life whereas he, in his retirement, was dreaming of going for a walk in an area covered with trees, watching their colours, listening to the birds and taking in the nature that gave him peace. Could he not realize that looking always to the end changed nothing in life? Did he feel that giving up on the daily pleasures and worries took him nowhere? Looking around him at the younger generation he felt that his attitude towards life – or the end of it – did not help them in their work and bringing up their children.

After spending some time with the couple, he started looking back on his life. They were keen on describing to him their discoveries around the world and the beauty of their contact with other countries and human beings. The acquisitions they brought back with them kept in their mind the rich variety of the human values that were so different from their own world. They seemed to feel his problem without talking about it and they did their best to get him out of his hole. The uneasiness that he felt going around the house did not leave him and being convinced by their arguments did not help him change his outlook on life ... or its end.

Going back fifty years, Abe remembered the first time he

saw the woman. She had passed by their country on her way to the USA to enter university. She spent a week with them to see her sister, Abe's wife, and they didn't see her for the following twelve years.

Her second visit, which lasted less than a month, was quite turbulent. She travelled around the region to visit the neighbouring countries. Her studies had gone well and she was working in the field of her specialization but the problem that followed her without leaving her in peace was her failed marriage. She was separated from her husband and needed some contact with her past. On going back to the USA, she changed her job and moved to a southern state. Her new job teaching at a university gave her the chance to meet her second husband and their marriage was happy.

Her third visit followed after ten years. Her husband accompanied her and they were able to enjoy visiting the country. Their life went on happily and they had the chance to receive Abe and his wife many times. It was during the last visit – when Abe was already retired – that he experienced the feeling of uneasiness ... the couple tried their best to introduce him to their colourful life but it was not easy.

After that visit, Abe found out that the woman had to undergo surgery for hip replacement. This operation was necessary to enable them to continue their active life of running around the world and doing all that they usually did.

VIII

The two pictures that had been hanging in the home of Abe and his wife for the last four decades were inexpensive copies they had bought from a vendor on the banks of the Seine in Paris. It was their first trip to Europe and the main reason for the trip was to have an artificial eye made for Abe to replace the one removed when he had his cancer operation. The trip gave them the chance to visit London and Paris for three weeks and have a look at the world. They felt very happy during that trip in spite of the reason that led them to take it and they still had many memories of what they saw. All the travelling they had done since that time did not make them forget it. What led them to choose these two pictures was not clear but all the beautiful paintings they acquired after that did not reduce the place these two prints had in their hearts.

The first picture showed an old French worker with his wine bottle and cigarette relaxing after work next to a heap of excavated rubble with the shovel stuck in its middle. His boots as well as what remained of a loaf of bread were next to him. The picture was colourful while a vague grey outline of the Eiffel Tower was seen in the far distance. All the members of the family, including his children, were familiar with the picture, but the funniest question he heard about it came from his six-year-old grandson who knew nothing about its history. The boy wanted to know why the man had his boots off, and when Abe told him that the worker was probably tired and needed to rest after hard work, the boy wanted to know why there were no socks around!

The French worker, relaxing.

Don Quixote and Sancho Panza.

The second picture showed a black sketch of Don Quixote on his horse carrying his lance while his loyal companion Sancho Panza followed on his donkey. The picture was a simple cheap copy of the well-known sketch. All the same it was still there and it accompanied Abe to all the homes he lived in. It even went with his spirit to Spain, which he visited ten years later. When he was in Don Quixote's home town, the people there told him about a visitor who inquired about Carmen and the answer he got was 'ella e muerta'. But nobody there told him that Don Quixote is dead, for he still lived in the hearts of Spain's youth in the full force of his fantasy existence.

One of the remarks he heard from his daughter was funny. Upon seeing it hung on the wall, she commented that it was not acceptable to have the hero in a situation where the direction of his movement was facing a wall! There should always be a free direction for him to attack whatever he considered an obstacle in his pursuit of liberation.

Abe noticed in old age that his feeling towards these two pictures was changing with time. The people in them were dynamic at certain moments but they were inanimate at other times. This was easily understood in the case of Don Quixote, but it was also noticeable in the case of the French worker, who looked very keen on his drink at certain moments while at others the look in his eyes showed boredom. Looking carefully at the pictures, Abe doubted this change and wondered whether it came from within himself.

IX

Getting onto the shuttle bus at the airport, Abe was taken aback to see a thin, young, good-looking woman in the seat in front of him. The woman was quiet, sitting peacefully, watching the people coming onto the bus. Her face had a thin sheet of sadness over it, but she was smiling occasionally while looking from the window at the glowing October afternoon fading into purple twilight.

The woman's face took him back fifty years to his home country, when he had met a young German ballet teacher who had left her country during the Second World War to spend a few years in Italy before coming to the Middle East. The ballet teacher was good looking and her beauty was quiet; it left the impression of somebody entering a new world that she had been looking for and making up her mind to stay there. Her smile looked as if she was on the point of saying something but usually nothing was said.

Abe knew nothing about her family; it didn't occur to him to ask about her background and he took it for granted that she would remain in the Middle East ...which did not happen. What led him to meet her was the fact that many of the young girls he knew at the time had started attending the classes she gave in her studio and his wife's sister was one of them. The last time he heard about her was when his sister-in-law on a visit to Germany the previous summer, found out that the ballet teacher with whom she was constantly in touch by phone, did not want to be visited by anybody in her old age at home. In her eighties, what physical state was she in?

During the five decades since he first got to know her, there were many memories that were entwined with their life and with what was taking place in the region. All these memories passed in front of Abe's eyes as he sat in the shuttle bus behind the young woman. Her quiet peaceful smile brought them back to his mind, mixed with the colour of the foliage on the trees, with their branches moving in the wind, and the noise of the traffic that he couldn't separate from the continuous hum in his ears caused by his hearing problem.

His sister-in-law followed the career of the ballet teacher all through her stay in the Middle East. Their relationship went beyond the ballet lessons to become a part of her life there and nobody thought that what took place later on in the country would lead her to leave and go back to Germany where she did not seem to have a big family. In fact, her stay in the Middle East led her to adopt some of the habits and dreams of the local people. Abe remembers her inviting them once to attend a celebration by one of the well-known poets who recited beautiful Arabic poems about the dreams of the population, although she did not understand the language!

When, after the beginning of the civil war, the situation led her to quit, she left her studio and her belongings in the care of Abe's sister-in-law. During her absence, which they believed would be short, those who did not leave spent the time waiting and watching the days go by like the trees in autumn moving with the wind and the colours of foliage reflecting the sun, but the waiting time was not that beautiful.

Abe remembered accompanying his sister-in-law once to check on the studio. Everything was in its place, the mirror covering the wall of the main hall reflected their figures while the bars fixed to that wall brought back the pictures of the students training during their lessons. The books in the study were covered with dust since nobody touched them. When the absence had lasted a long time, the rent of the studio became a burden and it had to be evacuated. Abe remembered his sister-in-law moving its contents to the basement of her home, taking care to keep everything in good condition.

The civil war dragged on. Time passed and the movement of the tree branches in autumn continued. The contact by phone did not stop and the news from the teacher informed them that she had started to give lessons in her country, still waiting for the time when the old life could be taken up again.

At last his sister-in-law's children joined their father in the USA where he had started a business to keep the family going and she had to close their home and follow them. The furniture and equipment of the studio were still in the basement, so she had to liquidate the furniture and, wanting to pack the equipment to take with her, she discovered that a good part of it was rotten, the humidity had taken care of it. What was still in good condition was packed with her belongings and shipped to the New World.

All through the following years, the contact by phone continued. The branches of the trees with the colours of foliage in autumn continued to move in the new country and the expectation of a renewed meeting did not evaporate, until the previous year, five decades after having met for the first time, Abe's sister-in-law had the unhappy surprise of knowing that the ageing ballet teacher did not desire anybody to visit her and see her state!

Abe was still on the shuttle bus watching the young woman sitting in front of him. He wondered about her life and whether she was about to say anything as her smile implied. She continued to watch the trees moving in the wind. Did she have any idea how many years her presence took Abe back in time? Or what the state of the old ballet teacher was like?

Anyway time passes and Abe would always remember the young woman on the shuttle bus, but what he regretted was not having had enough courage to talk to her and take her back with him half a century – before she was born – to discover a woman who looked like her and who could not finish a trip she had taken.

The ghost of loneliness, 1986.

One Way

I

Abe spent most of his life running away from the ghost of loneliness. He worked hard and did his best – together with his wife – to give their children what he felt he had missed during his early years. He put on a jolly face in an effort to cheer them up whenever they were bitter or felt unfulfilled.

One evening he went back in time to an outing he had with his son Willy during Abe's first visit to the country where the latter was finishing his postgraduate studies.

During their dinner, he noticed that Willy was watching him quietly. Asking him what he was thinking of, the answer he got was: 'I am thinking of what I am going to look like thirty-seven years from now!' (Thirty-seven was Abe's age when Willy was born.)

Later on, he followed Willy being there for his own children growing up. For Abe, this person was a completely new revelation.

II

Abe always had a special feeling whenever he thought of a funny experience he had in the recovery room after an operation. Coming back to consciousness from anaesthesia was dominated by the memory of hearing the nurse telling him to take a deep breath and then to inhale successively until he was fully awake. While he was following these instructions, the nurse caught his hand going up to his face and she had to pull it down a number of times. It was useless asking him why he did that while he was not fully awake.

At that time he had to undergo an operation to remove one of his eyes because of a tumour. Before he was admitted to the operating theatre, while still on the stretcher, the surgeon came to him trying to encourage him. Abe, who was already convinced of the necessity of the operation, was obsessed by one worry that he communicated to the doctor. He wanted to be sure that the surgeon would not remove the good eye. The surgeon did his best to pacify him, even putting a big mark next to the eye to be removed, but this was not enough for him and when he started taking the anaesthetic, he was still reminding the doctor of his problem.

Waking up in the recovery room, he followed the nurse's instructions about breathing deeply but he could not prevent his hand from going up to his face to check the remaining eye. Unfortunately both eyes were bandaged and he remained restless until they removed the bandage from the good eye two days later.

The good eye, the bad eye ... these terms were of interest to him. What had the bad eye done to be called bad? Was its hidden tumour a punishment? For Abe the two of them existed and the role of the bad eye continued to bother him.

When the tumour was discovered, Abe started getting resigned to the idea of leaving this world. Now that they had told him he was saved, he had to start all over again ...

III

It was a beautiful autumn day and the sun was shining when Abe and his wife went by train to visit their daughter living in another state. The trip took twelve hours, mostly across green pastures and small towns. It was interesting to watch the different types of people getting on to the train and leaving it at different stops. Very often there were cemeteries along the track, but somehow the people did not seem to pay attention to them. They all saw them but apparently very few considered that one of these days they would be ending up there.

For most people, death is not a human experience. They are born only to live from day to day!

The sight of the cemeteries brought back to his mind the pleasant comment of an old man who went to a cemetery to choose a place for a tomb. He found a plot that he liked and when the person accompanying him said it was too crowded, the answer he gave was: 'Maybe, but that just means it won't be as lonely!'

During the long time on the train, Abe dozed off from time to time. He found himself out upon a vast empty plain, where nothing seemed to have happened yet and at the same time everything seemed already over before it had begun.

He started thinking of an old friend who was the director of a big hospital in town. Abe used to go to him whenever he needed anything from that hospital. Once, on coming back from a long trip, Abe was told that the man had undergone major surgery to remove one of his lungs. Going to visit him at home, Abe found him in good shape, keeping himself busy with one of his numerous hobbies. They spent a pleasant morning together, talking about everything except the operation. It was useless trying to find something different in his behaviour. All that Abe could see was a vague look on his face whenever he talked about the postgraduate studies of his children and the country they would ultimately reside in. This man had always had a problem with emigration and could not conceive of any of his children following a pattern of life different from his. The problem with his lung did not seem to have changed his attitude. Abe realized that the man's long career and the countless number of people he knew put him in a world that was not easily discarded, but his situation after the operation did not permit that way of life to continue. The only continuation, for him, was to direct his children in the same way and to continue his life through them.

When the man's wife joined them after her working hours, Abe started searching for a different look in her eyes. The woman, who was beautiful, had always been friendly with them and Abe was surprised to find himself searching for that different look. Of course he could not find anything but, all the same, he felt the existence of an invisible wall surrounding the two of them and keeping others at a distance. That wall seemed also to separate them from each other to a certain extent. Her normal life full of activity could not be enclosed in her husband's cocoon, nevertheless they were keenly looking for something beyond the present and Abe had no way of following that look.

Coming back from his thoughts about his friend, Abe continued to watch the endless number of small homes along the track. The people moving around these homes seemed to belong to another world and he could not connect them to anything he could think of.

IV

Abe went once on Good Friday to a concert given by a visiting choir and an organist. The music as well as the singing drowned him in a world of melancholy that took him far away from his daily life. The choir had come to the country for the occasion, nobody knew them and their outstanding performance was a source of happiness for everybody. The hall was full, he came across many friends and acquaintances, but what attracted his attention was the age group of the people around. Most of them were middle-aged or elderly people; the young generation was a clear minority.

Watching members of the choir, he noticed that a large number of them were young. Although they were all following the conductor, every one of them had his or her own expression. Their voices were all in harmony with the songs, but their faces were so completely different expressing the individual worlds that came out during their singing.

Irrespective of the music and harmonious singing, their inner worlds were so different from each other and the strong stage lighting accentuated the expressions on their faces.

Upon finishing any song, their inner worlds would regain their places inside, leaving their faces as they were in normal life.

Abe was very touched by their expressions. Moving his eyes from one face to the other, watching the happy, sad or indifferent expressions on them, he was able to follow the choir's spirit that took him away to different worlds that could only be expressed by music.

V

Going to see Fady, an old friend in his eighties, after an interruption of four decades, was an enriching experience for Abe.

Fady – who was a writer – rarely left his home. Since his retirement, he was usually in his chair by the window, with his writing pad on the low table next to him, keeping himself busy writing. His place by the window did not change for a long time, but what he did besides writing changed a lot. He used to be a chain-smoker who always enjoyed taking a drink while working and could not conceive of changing anything he did, but old age and the state of his health had the upper hand in his battle with old habits. He was forced to give up all these pleasures after having paid the price.

When they got to know each other half a century before, Abe had been a young engineer in a government job and Fady had been in charge of the administrative section of the same department. Their desks were in the same room and that gave Abe the chance to meet Fady's numerous friends whenever they dropped in to see him.

Besides his job in administration, Fady was the editor of a cultural magazine published in the high school of the archdiocese in the capital of the country. Knowing Fady's liberal attitude and the type of writing in his novels, Abe was surprised to find him in that position. Apparently the archbishop in charge was liberal to a certain extent and he appreciated the editor's talents. Anyway, Fady stopped writing novels during that period and kept busy translating classical works of the last century to avoid provoking the establishment. This situation did not last long and he had to abandon that work and concentrate on writing his novels without having to take into consideration the opinion of the others. His job in administration continued, he married, had children who also married, his son studied medicine, went abroad for his specialization, came back, married and settled in the home country. In the meantime Fady retired and got into the habit of sitting next to the window writing his novels.

During that period, Abe had left his job and started working on his own. Gradually he stopped seeing Fady and the only contact Abe had with him was through the novels published by Fady that reminded Abe of the old times.

Four decades later, after closing his office and starting to write his memoirs, Abe went to see Fady in the same house of old times and offered him his first book of memoirs with a dedication referring to Fady's first book, which he had dedicated to Abe half a century before. They picked up their old friendship without getting lost in the details. Most of the people they used to know were not around any more and those who were still in this world were retired in different places. From time to time, during his visits, Abe met one of Fady's children who happened to pass by, but he did not know any details about their life. What attracted his attention was the fact that the daughter whom he met by accident was not interested in knowing anything about that past. All his children were very keen on doing anything Fady wanted. They were all grouped in the family home with their children once a week, but Abe felt completely isolated from their world.

Once Abe was invited to attend a play based on one of Fady's novels. His children were all there, but the isolation that Abe felt was still the same. The play was performed on one night only and the theatre was full. The people present did not seem to be interested in the play; they had come from different places to be present with Fady in an outing he was taking from his isolation that was actually an outing for each one of them. Abe noticed many of them going to the front row to salute Fady who was looking around trying to get back the old times and the relations he had with the people he knew. The spirits of the friends who were a part of his life before they had left the world were hovering around the place and apparently the people who were still alive were looking for them.

Fady's children looked after everybody but their enthusiasm had nothing to do with the content of the play. Somehow Abe felt they were giving their father a last salute, or at least one of the last! His poor hearing deprived Abe of the pleasure of following the acting so he started wandering, in his mind, among the people trying to capture the old times with Fady and connect them to the present.

Once, before leaving to visit his children in the New World, Abe called Fady to tell him goodbye. The voice that answered him was very weak as if it came from a different world. On coming back from his trip five months later, Abe found out that Fady had left this world. His spirit joined the group of friends who had left before him. It started hovering around the place while Abe tried again to capture the old times.

After hesitating for a short time, he called Fady's wife and went to see her. His hesitation was due to the fact that the family had never taken part in his previous visits when he was taken up with Fady trying to relive their old memories. During that visit he discovered new friends who were anxious to revive the old ties he had had with Fady. There was his wife, daughter and grandson who was already a young man. They seemed to know a lot about his relationship with Fady and the old times fifty years ago. Their enthusiasm about continuing his visits was very touching and he felt that the deceased man was present with them sitting on his chair next to the window with his writing pad ready for a new novel coming from the other world!

A Dream of Fifty Years

I

Fifty years are quite a long time, but the duration of the dream does not mean it was 'idyllic'. During the five decades of its duration, there were many ups and downs, many pleasant and bitter memories, but what was clear about it was that it had a beginning and an end. Before the beginning, there were two decades of looking forward to it, and after the end, there was nothing left of it. The clear cut of the end does not deny its beauty with all its colours.

II

Discovering the nature of the dream dawned on Abe while he was going through a beautiful collection of photos about his native country between the years 1880 and 1914, before he was born. This collection had nothing to do with his own experience in the home country. It also had nothing to do with what he expected to find anywhere in the world. It simply showed a beautiful place, rich in its human variety and the collection of ethnic populations always preparing batches of immigrants to export to the outside world. What these immigrants – not excluding his own family – found in the new countries, besides making a living, was different in every case, and the satisfaction or deception of any individual depended on what he had left behind, and the nostalgia he had carried in his luggage.

III

Preparing himself for the dream had nothing to do with the beautiful depiction of the scenery and the different human elements shown in these photos. He was not aware of that during the two decades preceding it. Preparing for the dream was inspired by the nostalgic memories of the immigrants living around him during that period and by his obsession with the life in the home country with which he was not familiar. It was encouraged by his feeling of alienation in the country where he had spent his youth.

At the end of his life, the enchanting memories he has about his youth in a country of immigration have nothing to do with what at the time was his one-way obsession with a home country he didn't know. Now that the whole thing is behind him, he can sit quietly looking at the beautiful photos in the

His children in the village, 1964.

album that he discovered after the end of his life experience.

The photos, besides showing the scenery, depict the different cultures of the various communities grouped in a very small area to convey the beauty of differences, as well as the strife of minorities to continue living in a tiny country that barely exists.

IV

The fifty years that Abe spent in that dream were taken up by an active career and a family to bring up.

His children had a happy life. When they started going to school, the three of them had the same kindergarten teacher.

She was a part of their life and became a good friend of their parents. Abe and his wife remained on friendly terms with her and her husband many years after their children had graduated from university and travelled abroad. When this teacher retired, she moved to live in a suburb where Abe and his wife continued to visit her until they lost touch with her many years later after her husband had passed away and they started travelling very frequently to visit their children. Apart from their children's schooling there was an endless number of problems both personal and public, as well as the pain of seeing the people around them leave to go to other places or simply leave this world!

At the end nothing remained of the dream except a clear view of a problem he had to face in the cage without bars that surrounded his inner world all his life.

V

The dream continued to exist for other people without having the same ingredients or colours. He went on watching the photos that made him discover the nature of the dream, thinking of the collection of the different human elements that did not really alienate him from his home country

The alienation started with his feeling the demographic change around him as well as the departure of all his family. Going to live in another country was not the solution to a problem that originated from his inner world. Being next to his children wherever they were kept him in touch with his grandchildren. The relationship he had with them was close and they were always discussing their problems with him, but their world was not his world and their friends had a different outlook on life, besides the fact that their studies took up most of their time. Ultimately they would have their own lives somewhere else and he could not see himself running around the world to follow them.

The life he had with his life companion, wherever it took them, was the only reassuring part of the dream, hoping that he would not have to face a new choice before leaving this world!

Santo Again

It was not easy for Santo to get used to the idea of his two daughters going without him on a visit to their native country in the Middle East after an absence of eleven years in Australia.

The girls had finished their university studies and were preparing to start their careers but nostalgia for the homeland and the extended family did not leave them in peace. The two of them were operating during that time as if they were a single person, sharing a single dream, a single silence and a single apprehension. Their parents were expatriates who still lived – in their souls – the old life at home; they understood anyone who had ever felt like a foreigner. Their meals and their actions were only a shadow of what had already happened at home, a lagging ghost of where they really belonged. All the same they felt that their life in immigration was better off and that their daughters had an education they could never have been able to give them back home. Their daughters did not belong to the old country, but their feeling of being lost was getting stronger with time, as all events that happen are never ever over.

After arriving in their home country the two girls stayed with their uncle who gave them the chance to lead the royal life of tourists, visiting the historical sites and the beautiful mountains, all free of charge. Did they try to guess what their life would have been like had their parents remained in their old small house with their aunt and their grandmother? Did they try to guess the quality of education they would have had? Looking at their cousins' lives could have given them the answer ... but the girls did not have the time or the chance to contemplate all that. Their stay was taken up by the tours and the family invitations.

Far away, Santo was thinking of them all the time and when Abe called from America to inquire about the family, Santo conveyed to him his worries about the girls, knowing all the same that he could not be in their place. At the same time he did not fail to bring up the memory of the three decades he had spent working with Abe. Besides thinking of his family, Santo repeated the dream of having the chance to meet Abe at least once during the coming years, a dream that they both knew would not materialize ...

Thinking of the girls, Abe remembered their early years in the home country.

At the time he never had the chance to be close to them, their primary education was far from his world and their family life was a part of Santo's. The numerous problems that submerged the country during that period did not leave him a chance to think of other things.

After their emigration to Australia, he was always thinking of Santo and his work, without inquiring about the children's education, taking it for granted that they would follow the pattern of all the immigrants' lives. Later, Santo started telling him about their doing well at school and university. A new image started taking shape in Abe's mind and he discovered girls he didn't know starting interesting careers, the eldest in business and the second in law, with scholarships helping them to do whatever they felt like doing. At certain times, when Abe called wanting to talk to Santo, one of the girls took the line, and he noticed an eager voice that seemed to recognize him, telling her father that Abe was on the line. He did not have the chance to talk to them. What would he have told them?

Did they belong to the new country? Did they feel their father's yearning for his old life at home? Did they fully realize what the social security system in the new country had offered them?

Abe dreamed of what they would discuss together in a meeting that would never take place. He was constantly thinking of the young girls whom he knew as children without ever talking to them. He wondered about their children, the third generation expatriates, what would they keep of the old life their grandparents continued to live? Would they be able to refer themselves to any space, region, culture or nation?

The girls saw the ambition that propelled their father across the world. In a few years they would make their way alone. Their achievement might be quite ordinary, still there would be times when it would be unbelievable!

Obituaries

I

When Eddy passed away, Abe felt Eddie's leaving was the natural conclusion of everything that happened to his family. He continued the family's legacy of loss which, in a way, could turn out to be a legacy of freedom as well. He felt without any connection to life and when Abe started writing a story about him, he followed the different sentences that described his personality until Abe finished and wrote 'The end'. Then he felt scared ...

The remaining members of his family did not see Eddie's journey around them and did not feel the presence of his spirit. The journey took him around all the people he knew. It was dark as if the electrical power was off and he was feeling lost. When he stared at the glassed shop windows to see his reflection ... he saw nothing.

II

The last time Abe called to inquire about Sany's health, her husband took the call. He was crying as he said that he couldn't have a long conversation because Sany was passing away at that moment.

A film of her life whizzed through Abe's mind. She was one of their best friends, whom they had got to know forty years before and were happy when she met her life companion in their home during a New Year's evening. This took place a short time before Abe discovered that he had cancer in one of his eyes and Sany was around when he had his operation. Her smiling presence was one of the encouraging things at the time and, ever since that occasion, Abe could not remember her face without the smile. Her smile was rather sad, it traced back to her ancestors who were the leaders of a small religious sect. Their followers were always around them seeking their spiritual guidance.

Abe remembered meeting her father once and he could not forget the peaceful feeling left by the man. But it was like a pilgrimage back through time, the whole set-up was like a house supported by the past, and the past was dead.

Abe and his wife were on close friendly terms with the couple. Sany's husband started a successful business in town, they had their first two children and then the civil war broke out. They left the country and started roaming around to end up in London where the man, who had a flair for business, settled down with a very successful industry, and they started touring the world during their holidays.

The last time that Abe met Sany was on the occasion of her daughter's wedding in their home country three years ago before she started her series of operations. After that, he did not have the chance to see her, but whenever they talked over the phone, he felt that her voice could not have come from a face without that smile.

Her sickness at the end got all her children around their parents, they were always leaving their work in the USA whenever her state was critical to be near her. She was operated on in different countries and, whenever she had the chance during a phone call, she described her adventures to Abe and his wife with the same positive spirit without complaining about her suffering.

When Abe, after retiring, wrote his first book about the quest for belonging, he was very hesitant about sending her a copy, considering it to be depressing for a person in her state. All the same he sent her the copy. A few weeks later, on coming home from a trip, he was told that she had telephoned wanting to talk to him. He immediately called her back and was very happy to hear her telling him, in her usual voice, that she had read the book and found it encouraging for a person in her situation. It made her feel that there are many reasons to feel bad and she had identified with the suffering of a number of the people in the book. During their subsequent calls, she was curious to know whether he was writing another book and wanted to know whether it was 'insightful'.

At the time, she paid little attention to world news; instead she was listening to past conversations moving through the house in the thick silence surrounding her. She spent a lot of time listening to music and watching the leaves change colour in their garden. At the end, when she was in a coma most of the time, Abe's wife happened to call when she was awake. The conversation they had was pleasant as usual and her husband was surprised to know of that conversation that took place during a short waking period.

After her death, her husband told them that she had never lost hope and was always asking for things that could help her cope with her state. Even during the last weeks of her suffering, when they had to carry her from the bedroom to the hall downstairs, she was wondering whether it was possible to install an elevator on the railing of the circular staircase to help her come down!

She was buried in their native country. Abe had the chance to meet all her children as well as the rest of the family and it felt sad to see them all without her. The memories that kept flashing before him about the four decades of their friendship were dominated by a feeling of sincerity. This feeling was more pronounced whenever they passed through difficult times during illness and the civil war, her presence shedding a soft light on their problems.

All the people she knew felt the timelessness of grief: it seemed as if their beloved person had died only yesterday.

All the love she created was still there, all the memories were still there. She lived on in the hearts of everyone she had touched or nurtured while she was here. She influenced the people who were close to her from beyond the grave and they all followed her habits and tried to do what she liked. Death ends a life, not a relationship ...

After that Abe started coming across her during his wandering in the labyrinth. She did not talk to him, nor did she try to talk to anyone around her, but the sad smile on her face was always there.

Abe was overcome by the sadness and beauty of those moments, he had a sudden sense of irrevocable loss; the happy close friendship of early years, gone ... the beginning of his career ... the childhood of their children ... all gone!

A new chapter in the book of his human experience had begun, probably one of the last chapters.

III

It was an unpleasant surprise for Abe to come across Sam in the labyrinth. The man had the usual sarcastic smile on his face and, of course, it was not possible for Abe to talk to him there.

They had not met for two decades since Sam had left the home country during the civil war. Abe had received no news about him and did not know about his heart trouble. Apparently, the pacemaker they had given him failed and he passed away. Sam, who was their family doctor before the war, had left the country to reside for a short time in London before emigrating finally to the USA with his wife and children. The man had a very pleasant sense of humour and his medical consultations were always accompanied by stories of all sorts.

Going around in the labyrinth, Abe saw Sam with his sarcastic smile that never left his face. Going back to old times,

Abe was surprised to discover that the rich collection of memories he had about the man were dominated by a single incident that took place during the general assembly of the golf club in which they were both members. Sam, who didn't seem to approve of a certain item on the agenda, was standing calmly saying that the item in question was not 'commensurate' with the policy of the club. His comment was accompanied by his usual sense of humour. Now, three decades later, it is surprising to remember him pronouncing the word 'commensurate' without remembering the subject of the discussion.

During his professional career before emigration, Sam was doing very well, his wife came from a big and wealthy family, but he felt an outsider belonging to a population reduced to the status of refugees. Was this a premonition or the real state of not belonging? One cannot say ... it seemed symbolic of his whole life. His set-up in the country where he lived before emigration, in spite of his success, resembled nothing so much as a house before someone moves in. Whenever Abe visited him in his home – before his emigration – Sam went back with his memories to the origin that was not wiped out by a successful career and a big family. He seemed to live in both eras at the same time and he smiled sarcastically as he brought back the ancestors he felt he was still living with, and all that was not 'commensurate' with his successful career.

After emigration, he did not try to practise his profession. He led the artificial life of all the immigrants around, every one of them trying to retain old habits. Coming here they at least maintained the illusion of making their own choice. As

Sam stood watching the attitude of all the immigrants, he realized – although they did not – that he was at the end of something. He knew that these days would soon pass and that these people, as well as their kind would also pass. Caught between birth and death, doubt and belief, evil and good, his sarcastic smile was all that was left of his memory.

Whenever Abe passed by the building where Sam had his clinic in the home country, he could not help seeing the sarcastic smile that accompanied their friendship and the word 'commensurate' kept on ringing in his ears.

IV

When Abe lost his uncle Nassim by death, he suddenly felt that 'Eden' without the graves was no longer 'Eden'. His uncle's grave was not there! Nassim had passed away during the civil war and he was buried in a place far from his family's village where his presence was always felt in all social and religious ceremonies. A 'voice' comes from where he was buried calling for the graves of his village, trying to remind everybody of his being far away …

The last years of Nassim's life were stamped by his becoming deaf. The smile on his face was a part of his personality all his life. After becoming deaf, he did not harbour any curiosity about what was being said and maybe he felt it was pointless to hear anything. He gave up trying to hear any news and lived in a world of his own.

Abe felt very bad when he had to avoid telling Nassim about

the death of his sister and nephew in their country of immigration in the Middle East, as well as his brother's death in the Caribbean. During those two occasions, Nassim sat smiling quietly with the people who came to pay their condolences, and Abe could never tell what passed through his uncle's mind seeing all the people around without knowing the reason for their visit. For Nassim, their presence carried with it the ghosts and shadows of all the possible reasons for their visit, all the unknown alternatives that could have explained it but did not.

Later on, after his uncle's death, Abe kept on hearing that 'voice' asking about his sister, his nephew and his brother without getting an answer to the questions.

Going around the labyrinth, Abe came across his uncle with his quiet smile and a sudden awful clarity about the questions that the 'voice' had raised. Nassim had discovered in various rooms of the labyrinth the people he had missed, his sister, nephew and brother. They were already dead. It was useless giving any explanations, there never had been any talking in the labyrinth. Getting out of the labyrinth, Abe heard the 'voice' raising new questions about the deceased people's graves as well as a place for his own grave, all far away from Eden.

Going back fifty years, when Abe came to settle in his parent's country, Nassim was always around and his affection for his nephew was clear. He followed the family's growth and was happy when his sister and his other two nephews came to see them during the summer holidays. A pleasant memory that Abe still has about that period was of an afternoon in summer while Abe and his wife were reading peacefully at home in their village. Nassim dropped by and asked them whether they were preparing for an exam the following day! He saw no other reason to explain their reading.

He did his best to help his nephew when Abe received his brother at home for medical treatment after his paralysis, and was available to do any service whenever Abe needed him.

The most painful memory that Abe kept from that period was when Nassim lost his eldest son who was killed in his home by a bomb during the civil war. The son was living with his family in a different village and Abe witnessed the effect of that tragedy on his uncle. When they got the son for the funeral and burial in their native village, Abe was taken aback to see Nassim – in spite of his total despair – insisting on keeping all the habits and respecting all the traditions of the village population during the funeral. For him, his son's grave was in their village where he could visit it and pray in front of it. This continued until the civil war reached 'Eden' and the cemetery was destroyed.

Nassim's care for traditions, in spite of the sorrow he felt, came back to Abe's mind when the man passed away in a different village and was buried as an unknown person. The 'voice' that came from where he was buried continued to haunt the family members. It was present during all the funerals that took place after that, even when the deceased people were not buried in their village. 'Eden' without the graves was no longer what it was ...

When Abe looked out of the window every day, he noticed the change in the trees, how strongly the wind was blowing. It was as if he could see time actually passing through the window-pane.

V

Sitting quietly in the main hall next to the church, Abe was watching the large number of people coming in to attend the funeral of an old acquaintance of his. The line of people passing in front of him was long and it was interesting to study the behaviour of every one of them. They were all well dressed and most of the ladies were in dark clothes. There seemed to be a lot they had to tell each other while waiting for the memorial service to begin. Abe recognized a number of the people around but he was not interested in getting up to talk to any of them. The films of similar situations passed before his eyes and the repetitive pattern of the occasion started to become boring.

The deceased man had committed suicide after living through many years of health problems. He left a note to his family telling them about his intention. The crowd of people present were all aware of the fact and were curious to know more details. The trauma of his suicide petrified them all and they recounted it in different versions. They also spent the time watching the man's widow who was a friend to them all. She looked as if she was standing in a pool undressing the days, removing the layers of events and incidents so they would no longer be within her.

The last months had been very difficult and probably the dead man had not supposed that his family would bear his senility more happily than his death.

VI

It was a nice surprise for Abe and his wife to see Tony's pleasant pretty face in a popular restaurant after an absence of two decades. Tony had been their neighbour for a long time in the same building until the civil war led them to change their residence many times.

When they met at the restaurant, she was talking in her usual excited voice but what surprised them was seeing all her family sitting seriously around her. Her eldest son who had emigrated to Canada was present, his younger brother who was working in a local technical firm was also there as well as their father. Somehow, her pleasant talk seemed quite strange compared to the attitude of the others.

Sitting at a table next to Tony and her family, they started exchanging their news with them and it didn't take a long time to discover that she was under treatment waiting for a major operation and eventually an unknown future. Tony was in her fifties at the time and was very anxious to resume their old friendship. She invited them to spend an evening in her new home, which was not far from theirs.

After that evening, they started making plans to resume their meetings and rebuild their relationship. All these plans were shattered when she went in for her operation, her health started getting worse and eventually she passed away.

Going back to the old days, Abe remembered an old story when he was on a visit to Cairo during the New Year's holiday. He dropped in to see Tony's mother and gave her a letter that Tony had sent with him. The mother wanted to send with him a number of presents to her daughter but there was no time to go and buy any, so she gave him a collection of cakes that had remained in her home after the feasts. Abe was not prepared to carry with him all the cakes that her mother gave him but he did not want to refuse, so he took them and gave them to the doorkeeper where he was staying. On coming home, he told Tony about the present from her mother and asked her to thank her mother claiming that she had received it. All this took place with the usual pleasant sense of humour that accompanied Tony all her life ...

After her death, Abe did not see her husband very often. Passing by his shop from time to time, it was difficult to bring up Tony's memory and it was not easy to find any other common subject for their conversations. A few months later – when Abe could not drive his car anymore – he was once standing in the road waiting for somebody to give him a lift when Tony's husband passed and stopped for him. The way to town was quite long and they could not help bringing up Tony's story. The husband came out with his grief. He told Abe that life for a widower was very sad, no day passing without his dreaming of old times, Tony's shadow accompanied him all the time and mainly at night.

Abe was taken aback by the man's total sorrow and could find no other subject to talk to him about.

VII

The sun splashed through the foliage as he walked in the green

Walking, with the dry leaves crunching under his feet.

area covered by high trees hiding the homes in the neighbourhood. Such walks dispersed melancholy and Abe enjoyed going alone for a walk, especially when the feeling of sadness resembled the mist overtaking the rain.

He was spending a week with his relatives in the south of the USA, and he felt the need of being on his own walking around. With his problem of slight dizziness when he moved quickly, he needed something to lean on, so he asked his brother- in-law who gave him a cane that had belonged to his late mother.

The walk was very pleasant as usual, the sound of dry leaves crunching under his feet making him feel at home. He started remembering scenes that took him across time back and forth. All of a sudden, he saw the old woman's ghost hiding behind the trees and going ahead of him wherever he went. Leaning on the cane to keep his balance, Abe felt it tickling his palm and directing him towards the ghost that was moving around among the trees. An image from the other end of time came to walk beside him on that morning, a new melancholy kept him company and he remembered the deceased woman, leaning on her cane, the last time he had seen her.

The woman was born and brought up in Egypt and lived there until she got married at the age of eighteen. During her early life, her family was friendly with Abe's family and she sounded happy telling him stories about that period when Abe was too young to remember anything. After her marriage, she moved to live in a town near Jerusalem where her husband – who was a doctor – lived until he passed away. Then she went with her children to Lebanon to join her husband's family. All through her life of more than eight decades, she kept the accent of her youth and did not try to change it. At the end of her life in Cyprus with her daughter, an image of that time accompanied her. Her mind seemed to be away somewhere else ... some other time ...

Abe closed his eyes and followed the lead of the cane and the parade of images that just continued to march in front of him. Hearing the comforting sound of dry leaves crunching under his feet, he met the old woman's sad stare from the photos of her son's wedding. It invaded his memory and he couldn't keep things straight in his head. A closer look among the trees, gave him more details about the deceased woman's story. She had changed her country of residence four times, but her first accent and the memories of her childhood prevailed. Slowly her pain reached every part of him. It hurt although all that he remembered about her face was the familiar friendly sensation and the stories she had told about his family when he was born. The stories meant nothing to the others, her children and grandchildren were not in this world before she got married.

All the stories were stored in the memory of the cane so that the old woman did not carry them to be buried with the past. They were there for people who had access to that memory ... or was it access to the 'hard disc' of the cane?

Returning from his walk, Abe felt more familiar with the cane, which was so far from the world of the second generation of that family. It looked livelier and seemed to have its own life in the stand where other canes and umbrellas were stored next to the entrance of the house. Whenever he happened to pass by that stand, Abe did not fail to see the old woman's ghost and a certain twitching in the knob of the cane ... and that always sent him to the past!

VIII

Telling his paralysed brother 'S' good-bye before leaving to go to work, left Abe with an overwhelming feeling of guilt. He saw 'S' gazing at him with an imploring look in his eyes that expressed his inability to utter a single word.

His brother was 52 years old when he suffered the stroke that ended a very active career. The memories that invaded Abe's mind were very painful. 'S', a very good-looking young man, was two years older than Abe and during their childhood and teens they had been close to each other. Abe still remembered 'S' at the age of fifteen standing in front of the mirror to comb his hair. He was singing a very popular song at the time and when he got excited about it he held the comb in front of his face like a microphone and forgot all about the combing.

Being in a hurry to go to work reminded Abe of his brother's successful career. There was nothing he could do about being busy although he could have stayed a little bit longer.

These memories started to invade Abe's mind when he retired ten years after the death of 'S' and he could not get away from the feeling of guilt. Avoiding staying longer had not only been due to his work; he had simply been at a loss what to tell his brother. He was ashamed of his busy career and could not stop to think back on their life together.

Their childhood was overwhelmed by the absence of their

'S' during his last visit, following a physiotherapy treatment, 1977.

father who died when they were in primary school. Being a small family of immigrants, their mother – who had a very good nature – had enough worries to keep her busy, and there were no other relatives to guide them, so they tended to have independent characters.

When Abe went to live in the home country and start a family, his contact with 'S' was reduced to his mother and brothers' visits during the summer holidays until 'S' had the stroke. Unfortunately this occurred at the beginning of the civil war in their home country. It was during that difficult period that Abe had to face the experience of leaving his brother to go to work. After that he did not have the chance to see 'S' except a single time when there was a lull in the fighting. During that visit, 'S' was in a better state and they got him to spend the summer with Abe and his family and to follow treatment for physiotherapy and speech therapy, but that was the end of their contact in life. After that visit 'S' had a second stroke that left him vegetating for eight years until he passed away.

There was an underlying odour of loneliness. Both 'S' and his younger brother did not get married, and when you are the last of your bloodline, you cannot help looking backwards as looking to the future shows an empty void. Their mother passed away one month after 'S'.

Abe's wife and his eldest son went to visit 'S' four years before he passed away but there was no contact with him. He was lying in bed manipulating the remote control of the television set without communicating with anybody around him. What did he see while watching television? He was probably building for himself a whole world with beautiful landscape and crowded towns where he could hear the echo of footsteps going nowhere, or out of this world, leaving the lost time and the lost places in a corner of his heart.

This was the last time that Abe's son saw his uncle before he passed away. It was also the only chance he had to visit the country where his father had spent his childhood and early years. It reminded him of the stories Abe used to mention from time to time about his family life before he got married. The whole thing was like taking a journey in the past. Did he manage to capture the spirit of these years? What memories did he carry with him back home and eventually to the new country of immigration? When would these memories come out to describe to his own children a world that was far from where they lived at present but quite close to the family world and the picture they had of his uncle whom they had never met.

The feeling of guilt accompanied Abe all his life and the imploring look of 'S' in his bed still haunted him whenever he thought of their childhood and of his brother singing in front of the mirror!

Before the Sun Sets

I

On his first visit to his native country, which did not last more than two months, Abe had to undergo an operation to remove his appendix. His cousin George, who was a well-known gynaecologist, took him to the hospital of a friend of his and the operation was performed under local anaesthesia. During the operation, Abe was able to follow the conversation between the two doctors and he was surprised to find out that they were having a long discussion about the political situation.

At the time all that he came across in the country was new to him: the village life, the big family, the social set-up, as well as the political situation. His cousin's role in public life was also one of the things that he discovered. This role was never brought up during that visit. All through the remaining years of his life – for more than thirty-five years – his cousin was very close to Abe, but he never brought up that subject.

After his death, when his memoirs were published under the title 'Before the Sun Set' Abe had the chance to discover George's role in public life.

II

When Abe was preparing to get married after coming back to settle in his home country – four years after that first visit – it was not easy to choose his best man for the wedding.

He had newly arrived at a place where he had no friends, in spite of the fact that his family was big, and the relatives were numerous. His childhood and school friends as well as his brothers were all in the country of immigration which he had chosen to leave, and he did not have the means to invite them over.

His choice of best man seemed strange to the others. The man – who was his cousin – was more than twice his age. He was a well-known gynaecologist, but Abe had no idea about his role in the public life of the country. Abe's feeling of closeness to this cousin went back to his early childhood after the death of his father. He always saw the letters George used to send them in their country of immigration but he did not have the chance to meet him until the age of twenty when he had the operation. These letters, apart from the usual greetings, concerned the plots of land owned by their deceased father that George managed to sell and transfer the money to their mother for their needs. This went on until the beginning of the Second World War when these transfers were no longer allowed.

Later on, Abe got to know that his father – who was George's uncle – had helped him to plan his life and enter university. He had needed to follow his uncle's advice since his parents were not educated enough to help him in this domain.

III

At the time of his wedding, Abe knew nothing about George's youth nor about the difficult years he went through until he managed to succeed. But of course, his cousin did not hesitate to accept being best man. George was pleasant during the ceremony. Not being a believer, he even asked the bishop officiating at the wedding to make it short and Abe noticed the cleric skipping a number of pages while reading from his book, so as to get the ceremony over in half an hour.

Their close relationship was never interrupted but the difference in age left an unseen barrier between them. Abe continued to go to his cousin whenever he needed a formality from any administration, and it was usually done without any problem. He never knew the extent of the influence the man had in that domain. Starting to look for work, Abe needed his cousin's recommendation for an opening as he did not know many people and had no other way to proceed. At the time the country did not have an organized system for employment, and one had to go through personal connections to find a job, provided that these connections were sincere.

The first attempt was in the private sector, and George sent him to the owner of a big firm who did not seem to be willing to take him. On entering the man's office he found him buried in his papers, and all Abe saw was the bald head of a man not bothering to look up, telling him that there were no vacancies at the time.

The second attempt was at the electricity company in the country. George knew the head of a department there who was the son of a medical colleague of his. The head of the department took Abe to meet the general manager who was French. The manager received him well, but after a few weeks the answer Abe got was negative. Twenty years later, when Abe was already a successful consultant, he got to know that the man who had taken him for the interview had a nephew about to graduate from France and he had in mind to get him employed there, so he told the general manager that Abe, who was a beginner, wanted to be named head of a main department and, of course, his application was refused. The following few attempts did not succeed and it was always the same problem, but he was never told frankly the reason for these refusals.

The last attempt was for a small government job and the head of the department that Abe went to see needed a young engineer with his qualifications. After the interview, the man told him that he would approve his being employed, but Abe had to find somebody who knew the general director of that ministry to accept his application. Again Abe had to go to his cousin who happened to know the general director well, and he finally got the job. This was the last time Abe applied for a job. He spent six years working hard for that department and then resigned to work on his own as a consultant, using the experience he had acquired during those six years.

IV

His first two children were born in his cousin's maternity hospital and he remembers that George was surprised when he found out that Abe did not name the first child after his grandfather.

When the two children were seven and five years old, Abe had to undergo the operation to remove his left eye because of a tumour. George again was present at the operation. He was worried and he did his best to find out the details about the problem without telling Abe what he found out. This, Abe discovered, when his younger brother – the physician – passed through in summer to see them. His brother had a long discussion with George, after which he told Abe about the pessimistic answers their cousin had obtained from the medical authorities he had contacted after the operation.

George had closed his hospital before the third child was born. He had stopped practising medicine and was spending most of his time writing. During that period Abe used to see him more often. It was interesting to talk about different subjects but, at the end, it became painful to notice the degeneration of his health. They talked about the George's children and Abe's brothers, but George never talked about his career or his role in the public life of the country. This had to wait until Abe read his cousin's memoirs after his death.

V

When George – near the end of his life – started writing his memoirs, it was normal to stand back to find himself outside the events he was commenting on in order to get a better view of them. His obsession with the past shifted its ground from historical facts to remembered time. The war years held the time back, and the different experiences he had became forums for the wisdom of old age.

In the village where George spent his childhood years happily, there were many difficult times, mainly when his father travelled twice to the New World to make enough money to support the family. His mother, who came from a bigger family, kept her children in touch with her relatives living in a neighbouring village, and George remembered spending the happiest days of his early years playing there. He enjoyed watching the meetings the elderly people held to discuss their daily problems, no matter how insignificant the problem was. He still remembered an amusing meeting of these elderly people when they were discussing the case of a young man from town who proposed to marry a girl of their village. They considered themselves all responsible for the girls of the village and they started telling each one of them to state his opinion until they decided – as was usually the case in such meetings – to leave the decision to the oldest man present!

After George finished primary school, his uncle had helped him to enter a secondary school in a distant town and it was then that he started his life as a border away from home. The school was of a good standard and, having graduated from it, he had no problem being admitted to university. To cover a part of his expenses, he began working at the university restaurant serving food to the other students before having his own meals. The unpleasant behaviour of a number of the wealthy students never left his mind to the end of his life.

VI

The memoirs were very long and clear, but Abe discovered – while reading them – that he was mixing what he was reading with his own memories about his cousin. At certain times he even mixed that with what had happened in his own childhood. There was no point of departure and no point of return and almost no point of continuity, an incoherence that passed and melted away.

After graduating from university during the First World War, with the famine in his country, George had to join the Turkish army and he was sent to different fronts and, being a medical officer, the experience he had there left a deep imprint on his character. He still remembered a young girl living next to him who was keen on having a relationship with a young man in spite of the conservative traditions prevailing, but she was discovered by an old woman and he never knew what the family did to her after his leaving that place. His work with the army at the time made it possible for him to send some help to his family during the famine.

At the end he was taken as a prisoner of war by the British army and put in charge of some hospital work on the Suez

Canal. With time his position became better and he was allowed – as a member of the medical corps of that army – to travel in Egypt to visit his uncle. He remembers once standing in front of his uncle's pharmacy in his army uniform when the people around attacked him as an enemy, but the neighbours who respected his uncle and knew about his status interfered to save him from their hands.

After the end of the war, George wanted to go to South America but he didn't have a chance to reach there. On his way the ship stopped at a town in West Africa where he had a close relative running a successful business. His relative – who apparently had news from the family – did not approve of George's plans; for him, it was out of question to lose the only doctor in their family, so he took him for a long drive in the countryside and when they came back the ship had already left the harbour. George was very worried about his shattered plans until he found out that his relative had arranged for him to go to Paris to finish his specialization. He gave him a good amount of money to start his life there and gave instructions to his correspondent in Paris to offer any assistance needed during the following months. George's studies went normally and he regained his native country to start his career.

He only succeeded after many difficulties. When he started practising in his village he discovered the hidden face of human nature. He had no problem with poor people who couldn't afford to pay him but he was shocked by the behaviour of those who had the means. The wealthy ones tried their best to exploit him and never failed to tell him that the doctors in town who came from rich families treated them in a better way, their coming to him was only a way of encouraging him.

VII

There was also the memory of George coming to visit once when Abe's mother was spending summer with Abe's family. The man was quite old at the time and the family was living on the fourth floor of a building that did not have an elevator. It was not easy to see him climbing the stairs slowly; with his smiling face and the onslaught of the final years of his life approaching. What Abe saw then left no place in the picture for the successful career and the prominent role in public life. It took him back over more than six decades to the village of George's family and the boy of the early years was there. The passage of years did not wipe out the happiness of that boy at his uncle's village and his amusement during the meetings of the elderly people discussing problems of village daily life!

The picture of George's young years was always present with Abe although he was not in this world at that time. It came up once when his cousin came to see him in the village after his appendix operation fifty years before. Abe's aunt, who was also George's aunt, was still alive at 95 and started talking about her children in South America and the chance of their coming back home to see the family. The dream of seeing her children back in the village never left her. It was surprising to see George talking to his aunt as if he was still the young boy playing with her children in the village and the image of happiness spreading over his face.

This image was also there when Abe went to see his cousin after the latter had retired. Their discussions usually covered many subjects, but Abe's career was rarely mentioned just as

George's career was ignored. At that time George's young daughter was living with her family in the storey that had been occupied by her father's hospital and he had kept a small area at the back entrance for himself. There he had his desk and a few chairs for the people who came to see him. There was a small balcony full of flowers and he usually sat there with his visitors when the weather was good.

There, George's distant memories were a part of the present in the quiet time that surrounded him. He had had a very busy life, he had travelled a lot around the world and the important events that he had witnessed were mixed up with the family relationships that Abe reminded him of. The image of his uncle came back with the images of the world leaders he knew …

The thing that attracted Abe's attention while reading his cousin's memoirs later was the period of his childhood. The whole book was very interesting and his cousin's career was outstanding, but the childhood years with the happy memories in the small village with all the relatives around reminded Abe of his own childhood years in a country of immigration without meeting a single relative before he reached the age of twenty. It is true that he had many school friends and neighbours but the vague nostalgia he had for a native country that he didn't know was stronger than the happy relations he had with all the people he knew in his early years. This nostalgia accompanied Abe all his life but was not enough to eradicate his feeling of missing the childhood friends, especially as he did not have the chance – during the long years of the civil war – to go for a visit to look them up.

One of the last memories that Abe kept of his cousin was

very sad. Once upon entering George's retreat he was bothered to see the man's face covered with sweat and his hand shaking while he tried to give himself an injection. What was that injection? It was pointless to ask. After a short time George was relaxed again and they took up their discussions as if the episode had not taken place.

VIII

At this point in his journey among memories, Abe strayed away from his cousin's memoirs to indulge in the stories of other people.

When he went to attend the memorial service of an old man he didn't know well, he was taken aback to discover what he had suffered during the last days of his life. The man was rich but Abe never had the chance to come near his inner world, and was surprised to hear the man's daughter talking about her father's last days. Apparently he had been very close to his wife who had passed away four months before him. His life during the last months was quite taken up by medical treatment and numerous surgical operations. His children rented for him a nice flat in town near the hospital since it was not easy to keep him in the beautiful house he had in the mountains. Whenever he was able to have a day of rest, he asked one of his children to take him up to his house where he asked for a cup of coffee, which he drank on the balcony watching the familiar scenery around. What did he think of during those visits? Did he spend time on the balcony with his wife? Was he apprehensive about leaving this world or did he want to resume the life he had with the person he loved? From having walked so far hand in hand, they could even agree to a rendezvous in the same dream.

It wasn't his own inevitable death that he couldn't understand, but all the other deaths that passed by him during a long life without making him wonder about the impermanence of all that exists in this world.

Nobody had the courage to ask him any questions and his slow trip out of this world had nothing to do with the busy life he had led before his wife had passed away. Abe was thinking of all the possible thoughts that could have passed in the man's mind on the balcony drinking his cup of coffee, but these thoughts did not seem to bother the people attending the memorial service. They were all wondering about the running of his big business and the distribution of his property.

IX

Going back to his cousin's life Abe remembered George's wife. She came from a well-known family and was very proud of it. She was around when Abe's children were born and she was very pleasant throughout. From time to time she invited him to a dinner party at home. During one of those dinners Abe met her cousins who happened to be the owners of a small electricity distribution company for which he had done a lot of consultations before. The discussions he had with these old clients were far removed from the relations he had with his cousin although they took place in the latter's house, and Abe noticed that his contact with his cousin was always a continuation of George's childhood and an anticipation of the memoirs that were to come.

Their close relationship did not erase the unseen barrier between them because of the difference in age and their different childhood experiences. All the same it opened the floodgates that had contained the past for so many years and the torrent of all that had lain hidden in the deepest layers of memory poured out without their talking about it.

The past that kept Abe bound to his cousin was always present in the different historical subjects they talked about, the different public occasions that were taking place, and the different things that had happened to their relatives.

In time Abe and his cousin approached the old times, each from his angle, and they kept up a relationship that never opened the family's history book, but still covered a certain phase of the life of a country to which each of them belonged in his own way. Sitting on George's small balcony after his retirement, they liked to listen to the dreams of the people around them and feel the breath of the young generation that shared with them the same country. They usually spoke in a low voice so as not to alter the silence of time.

Abe could not help the feeling that they were a tribe frozen in remote time.

X

The experiences that they had at the beginning of their lives were so far from each other that they left Abe surprised to find himself so close to his cousin. George's happy years in the village with all the relatives around and with all the ancestors present in the background gave him a certain sense of belonging and assurance that accompanied him in all that he did, both in his profession and in public life.

On the other hand, Abe's lonely years in a country of immigration – especially after losing his father – gave him a certain sense of alienation. The school years were pleasant, the friends around him were nice, but the feeling of exclusion never left him. He was always annoyed by any sign of compassion even from the poor workers who, in an attempt to show their respect, addressed him as a foreign citizen. The dream of belonging to a home country he had not seen never left him.

The unseen barrier between the two cousins was there for both of them. Abe could not avoid noticing that George, who was always ready to help him, hesitated before approaching his inner world. The barrier between them was actually a barrier surrounding Abe in spite of all his attempts to belong. Apparently when one is displaced once, one remains displaced for life.

XI

With time George started travelling a lot, and most of his trips were to the socialist countries. Apparently the stamp that was left in his memory of the difficult times he had passed through during his young years was not wiped out by a very successful career, and he wanted badly to believe the claims of the ruling parties in these countries about justice.

It was easy for him to believe those claims from a safe distance, with a very successful career at home and a big collection of friends and influential people around him, without having to submit to the regulations in those countries

In fact this firm belief started to shake near the end of his life when he started looking back to write his memoirs, but he did not live long enough to witness the collapse of his fantasy.

When an old man – in his eighties – discovers the fallacy of a certain dream, it is not easy to start all over again the journey of his soul across the time that has run by, and with all the people who are not there any more.